WHAT BEAR SAID

about Life, Love, & Other Stuff

Torchflame Books

Words and Pictures by
Jack Wiens

Text © 2024 Jack Wiens
Illustrations © 2024 Jack Wiens
All rights reserved.
No part of this publication may be reproduced or transmitted in any form or by any means, electronic or mechanical, including photocopying, recording, or any information and retrieval system, without permission in writing from the publisher.

Second Edition
Published by Torchflame Books, an imprint of Top Reads Publishing, LLC.
Vista, California USA
For information about special discounts for bulk purchases, please direct emails to: publisher@torchflamebooks.com

ISBN: 978-1-61153-038-4 (paperback)
ISBN: 978-1-61153-039-1 (hardcover)
ISBN: 978-1-61153-088-9 (ebook)
Library of Congress Control Number: 2024939556

Book design and computer production by Patty Arnold, *Menagerie Design & Publishing* www.menageriedesign.net

Dedication
To my children and grandchildren
... and to my dear sister, Cheryl

Contents

Introduction 4

Opening 6

Being Present 7

Friendship 23

Love 31

Forgiveness 43

Honesty and Communication 53

Grief and Loss 63

Prejudice 69

Loving the Earth 75

Meaning and Purpose 87

What Bear Said

By Jack Wiens

Introduction

As I've gotten older, my gratitude has grown for the host of teachers who have impacted my life, some as brief visitors and others as life-long contributors to my education, maturing, and healing. These dear ones have shown-up as spouse, children, grandchildren, friends, family, counselors, school teachers, writers, animals and other natural forms.

There is this passion in me to pass on the lessons learned, to attempt to distill the wisdom of those teachers, and make it easily accessible. I asked myself, "If I could leave a message to my grandchildren, what are the questions I would want to answer? What has been helpful, healing and inspiring to me on this journey?" I needed a friendly figure to represent the teachers without being preachy. I chose a bear.

It's no accident that I chose a bear. Actually, it's more like the bear chose me. Living as I do in Ashland, Oregon, at the foot of the Siskiyou Mountains, I have a steady parade of wild critters in my yard. It feels like I'm in "the wild" even though I'm two blocks from downtown. One morning I even had an adult black bear on my roof! Other bears have visited in broad daylight along with many deer, raccoons, wild turkeys, and an occasional skunk. I have blue jays who come to my hand for peanuts and peck on my kitchen window if I don't show-up promptly.

So, Bear is the loveable, wise teacher and friend to the boy. The boy asks questions about some tough subjects, like grief and loss, forgiveness, prejudice and so on. It was my son, after reading first drafts of the book, who encouraged me to include more of my own personal material. I have done that and as a result the boy relates my real-life experiences on his journey with Bear.

Growing up I was painfully bashful and quiet. I learned to entertain myself by drawing. My dream was to become an artist for a famous animation studio. That didn't happen, but art has played an important role in my life. It feels good, after illustrating many books for other people, to finally create a book with my own message.

Bear's answers are drawn from psychology, philosophy, and just good old common sense. I believe many of my teachers and guides had such an impact on me because they loved me. Their love felt unconditional. I didn't have to earn it. To me, this is the bottom line—the only thing that really seems to matter—how we love each other in this world, or fail to.

My hope is, as you choose to stroll with Bear in these woods, you find some comfort and inspiration.

⁓ Jack Wiens

I can't remember when it began, but Bear and I have been talking for a long time. I've had lots of questions and Bear has answered them. Some of his answers didn't always make sense until much later... but Bear has always been there for me.

Being Present

It was a fine day in the woods...

Which way are we going, Bear?

What Bear Said
The way is whichever way we are walking together.

Eventually, we came to a tree where Bear sat down, leaned back and was quiet...

What are we doing today, Bear?

What Bear Said

We are doing it already... enjoying this moment, experiencing what is right in front of us. If you get quiet and just breathe you will notice things you might have missed. Isn't it wonderful!

Bear, you know, sometimes I don't understand what you mean and I'm embarrassed to ask you to explain.

What Bear Said

You can always ask me to say something again with different words. Of course, sometimes I don't even know what I'm talking about! You can tell me what you heard and I can tell you if that was what I meant to say. That makes for a good conversation!

Bear, sometimes I can't stay in the present moment because I'm worrying about how I acted yesterday.

What Bear Said

If something you did is bothering you, ask yourself if there is anything you can do to make it better... apologize, stop doing whatever's bothering you, give back, repair, or clean-up something?
This is called "making amends." When you have done all you can do then it is time to let it go and forgive yourself.

But, Bear, what about when I'm worried about the future? Like when my family moves to a new place and I have to change schools again. I worry about whether the kids there will like me and if I'll like them.

What Bear Said

If you don't have any control over something, then all you can do is let it go, focus on the present, breathe in and out, and trust you will be able to handle whatever comes up. And, remember, you can ask for help.

A few days later...

Bear, when I was the new kid in class, I was shy and nervous. I sat quietly and waited for someone to talk to me. Then, I got an idea. I drew popular cartoon characters, and some I made up, on my notebooks and when kids saw them, they thought they were cool and asked me to draw some on their notebooks. There was a nice person who showed me around. Now we're friends.

What Bear Said

Well done! You did a brave thing putting your art out there for others to see. There was a chance they wouldn't like it, but an even better one they would! May I see your drawings?

On the next day...
　　Bear, why did it have to rain today!?

What Bear Said
I don't know, but if we choose to, we can dance away the disappointment.

On another day we came to a place where the trees had burned in a forest fire. I felt sad for the burned trees, but happy for all the ones that weren't burned...

Bear, do you ever feel happy and sad at the same time?

What Bear Said

Life is always a messy mixture and our hearts are big enough to hold a mix of feelings about it all.

Paying attention to our feelings is important so we can understand why we're acting the way we are. Oh, and tears are good for us whether they are happy or sad ones. There are almost always opportunities for both.

Nature can be quite harsh sometimes… but, life just keeps coming back!

Friendship

Bear, do you ever get tired of me and your other friends?

What Bear Said

Hmmm… I do like being alone sometimes, but without you, Jay, Raccoon and all my friends I would be quite lonely. It is true that friendship requires patience.

For example, dear Raccoon loves to visit late at night and tell me her stories. They are interesting, but sometimes just LONG.

And there's Jay, who can get very excited and loud, but he always speaks the truth from a higher perspective.

Oh, and there's Porcupine. Very kind and dear, but a bit hazardous to hug!

Bear, maybe it would be best not to hug Porcupine.

What Bear Said
Perhaps.

There's also Badger. It's very hard to be his friend because he is angry all the time. He growls fiercely at everyone. I love him from a distance.

One afternoon after picking berries we saw Elder Moose. After visiting a while, Bear asked me to pour our berries on a flat rock for the old moose to enjoy as we went on our way.

Why did we give Elder Moose all our berries, Bear?

What Bear Said

Someday when I'm old I will appreciate someone bringing me berries... and, it just makes me happy. He's my friend. There are always more berries.

The next day I remembered something
Bear had told me... when we love someone
we should tell them and tell them why...
so I got Raccoon and Jay and we went
and told Bear.

What Bear Said

Well, well, that was quite nice! Thank you
for speaking your love out loud.
It feels wonderful!

Love

On this day I was thinking of how much I loved these woods and Bear and all the critters...

Bear what is love? I heard a song that said,
"Love is the Answer."
I don't even know the question.

What Bear Said

Oh good! Love is my favorite subject!
We all need love. If you love someone you're kind to them, patient, understanding, forgiving. You want what's best for them.

Love is what you feel for your family and friends. Love holds us together, brings us joy and gratitude. It makes us want to do and be our best. We can't live without love.

Bear, does love change? This is hard for me to say, but sometimes I'm afraid my dad doesn't love me. He gets very angry and ignores me. He never hugs me or tells me he loves me. I think he's disappointed in me. I think he'd like me to be tougher, stronger, braver... I don't know what to do.

What Bear Said

Just because someone IS a parent doesn't mean they know HOW to parent. Maybe your dad wasn't shown how to love when he was growing up. Maybe the hurts inside cause him to act angry. He might be afraid to say what's in his heart. Your dad loves you, but doesn't know how to show or tell you.

You are young, but you can decide that who you are is okay. You can't be somebody else... and neither can your dad.

It's hard, Bear. I know.

Bear, I like my best friend's family a lot.
His father is big and strong, very kind and
gentle. He has rules and tells his son what
he expects. He shows him how to do things.
He's patient. He even takes time
to talk to me. My friend's mother taught me
how to draw faces and how to paint.
I like being at their house very much!

What Bear Said

It sounds like they are wonderful human beings! This reminds me of how sometimes someone comes to us with loving gifts. The gifts might be things our parent couldn't give us. These kind people might be in our life for just a moment or a long time. We might not realize what they brought us until much later when we look back.

Sometimes, Bear, I feel like my mom loves me so much she could never let me go, even when I grow-up. I want to make her happy, but, I don't know... can somebody love someone too much?

What Bear Said

Yes, it is hard for some parents to let their children go when the time comes. It is your wonderful gift to someday go out into the world and live your own life and be yourself. Your mom will be okay.

Remember, if you love someone so much you forget to take care of yourself or you can never say "No" to them, or you hold on too tight and never allow any space between you, or you allow the other person to treat you badly, that will be a problem.

In a good relationship, kindness and love go back and forth and there is enough space for each person to be themselves. There is trust and honesty. It is safe to disagree and to ask for what you need or want.

Bear, have you ever been IN LOVE?... because I think I might be. There's this girl at my school. I can't stop thinking about her. When I'm around her I can barely speak and I sweat and shake!

What Bear Said

Ummm... well... yes, I have been in love, but that's a story for another day.

Being in love can cause you to act rather strangely. You love your mom, but you're not "in love" with her. When you're "in love" your heart does flippity flops. You want to be with that person all the time. You want them to think you are wonderful. You want to hug and kiss them. You want to make them happy.

Yes, being "in love" is quite special, something for which to be grateful. And, honestly, I like it quite a lot.

Bear, you said once I should love myself. Is that really okay? And how can I ever love these freckles!?

What Bear Said

If you don't love yourself, it will be very hard to love anyone else.

Remember, as much as all the stars in the sky and critters in the forest, you have a right to be here. You are loveable. Treat yourself as you would treat your best friend. Respect your body. It works hard for you... and your freckles go very well with your hair.

Forgiveness

Bear, honestly, sometimes I don't even like myself, especially when I mess up something. I get so embarrassed!

What Bear Said

The only way to learn is to make mistakes. Everyone begins like that. Just say, "I will do better next time," then work on it. Shaming yourself is a waste of time. Just forgive yourself and move on.

Later, as we sat on a hill...

Would you forgive me if I really hurt your feelings, Bear?

What Bear Said

I would forgive you because I love you, but it might take a little while. I might need to go up on my mountain and be alone. Of course, it would help if you told me you were sorry.

What if I hurt your feelings again and said
I was sorry again, Bear?

What Bear Said

I might still forgive you, but it would be harder to trust you after that. Trust is very important in a friendship. If it gets broken it can take a long time to repair. Apologies don't mean much if the hurtful action continues. If you are truly sorry you work on changing your behavior.

One day Bear went walking without me...

> Bear, it hurt my feelings that you didn't wait for me.

What Bear Said

Oh, I'm so sorry! Thank you for telling me. I'm very glad you spoke bravely from your heart. If you hadn't spoken-up I would have had to guess why you were upset and I probably would have guessed wrong.

Will you forgive me?

Yes, I forgive you, Bear. I feel much better.

What if I couldn't forgive someone, Bear?
Would that be so bad?

What Bear Said

Well, when I don't forgive someone, it makes me grumpy and gives me a tummy ache.

Resentment builds up and I might act mean towards the person. The sooner I can forgive, the better. Oh, and when I forgive it doesn't mean I've decided what they did was okay. It just means I've decided to be done being angry. I'm letting it go so my tummy can feel better.

Honesty & Communication

One day Jay landed close to me and screeched in my ear. I told him he was too loud and he quickly flew away...

Bear, is it always best to tell the truth... even if it hurts someone's feelings?

What Bear Said

Just because you have a thought doesn't mean you have to say it. Some thoughts are just too hurtful and not helpful. What IS important is to be honest when you do speak so others can trust you. The more vulnerable you are, the more others can feel safe with you.

There ARE things that need to be said that might upset someone. This cannot always be avoided. When you have something hard to say, stick to what happened (the facts), how you felt, and what you need now. Don't say judgmental things, like the other person being good or bad, right or wrong. Just say how you feel, what you need or want--your request.

What does vulnerable mean, Bear?

What Bear Said

When you are vulnerable you are letting others know who you really are, even your faults and failures. You aren't pretending to be perfect. This invites them to be honest with you. And, yes, it is risky because they might not like the real you...but, they might love you, too!

Why is Badger so mean? He made Raccoon cry and that made me angry. I can get so angry, Bear!

What Bear Said

Badger's family wasn't very kind to him. He doesn't believe he's loveable. He pushes everyone away so they can't hurt him. Anger often hides some hurt or fear in all of us. We protect ourselves like Badger. It's much better if we can look inside and talk about what's hurting or scaring us.

We also can have true anger. If we or someone else are being treated unfairly, we can say we are angry. We can stand-up for what is true and fair. That is important.

Remember, a lot of anger often hides a lot of pain and fear.

Bear, what if I am talking to someone and don't
like what they're saying? What if I think
their ideas are just dumb?

What Bear Said

It's sad if someone is judged without being heard or understood. Everyone has reasons for their ideas or beliefs that make sense to them. Can you listen carefully enough with an open mind and heart to hear those reasons? Friendship or a good conversation only happens when two listen and respect each other. They don't have to agree.

Do we have to go there, Bear?

What Bear Said
We can't avoid it. Sooner or later everyone must go there.

Grief & Loss

Bear, what am I supposed to feel when someone I love dies?
When my grandpa died I was very mixed-up.
Some people at the church said I should feel happy
he had gone to a better place, but that just kind of made
me mad. I didn't want him to be gone. I felt sad and lonely.
At first, I couldn't cry, then later, I did.

What Bear Said

I'm so sorry your grandpa died. I know it hurts.
Remember when we found Little Sparrow
lying on the ground not moving and
we realized she had died?

What we felt then and what you are feeling about your grandpa is called GRIEF. Grief can feel like sadness, anger, loneliness, hurt, fear, love, numbness—all at different times or all at once.

Later, it can seem like the grieving is over, then it comes again like a sudden wave of feelings. Eventually, it's like a tender bruise in our heart.

We can remember what we enjoyed about the one who died and feel gratitude. Can you tell me some memories you have of your grandpa?

So, I told Bear my memories and
I did feel thankful.
And then it felt good to just sit
together, not talking

Bear, what if I didn't like a person who died?
What if they had been mean to me?

What Bear Said

It might be very confusing. You can love someone and be angry at them for how they treated you. You might even feel relief that they can't hurt you anymore. We all feel things for good reasons. The reasons aren't always entirely clear.

You might try writing a letter to the person who died, telling them exactly how you feel. You could read it to someone you trust.

Prejudice

I was noticing the color of Bear's fur one day...

Bear, why aren't all bears the same color?
I think your color is the best.

What Bear Said

It would be boring if all bears were the same. What if, in the woods, all the flowers were the same and there was only one kind of critter or tree? How sad. I believe if you knew any bears of a different color you would like them, too.

Hmmm... I suppose I would.

Bear, why can't us humans accept our differences? Some people I know call other races disrespectful names and say hateful things about them. That makes me sad, Bear.

In one school I went to my best friend was Black. We didn't care what color our skin was. We just liked each other and had fun. Why can't we all just get along?

What Bear Said

I'm very glad you're understanding everyone deserves respect no matter what color their skin might be, or what religion they have, or how differently they might live. Many people were taught their whole lives to believe negative things about different groups of people and it is hard for them to believe anything else. Prejudice is about judging a whole group without really knowing them personally. It's only in truly knowing a person that we can understand and accept them, and perhaps grow to love them.

Loving the Earth

We were in my favorite grove of very big trees. A very large tree had fallen over a long time ago. It was dead and rotting, but out of its trunk there were new little trees growing... and ferns and all kinds of plants and flowers!

Bear, this makes me happy and sad all at once again, but, mostly, it makes me feel kind of peaceful.

What Bear Said

Yes, isn't it so wonderful how even this
dead tree is giving life to new ones. This is the
cycle of life and death, loss and growth, that
is always happening in these woods
and the whole world. These wise old trees
have strong life energy they quietly share
with us. Each one is unique and yet are all
connected underground by their roots.
They have survived fires, storms, droughts
and diseases. Everything in this natural
world is connected by this life energy.
It is in you, me and every living thing.

I wish this day would last forever, Bear.

What Bear Said

Yes, but tomorrow might be even better...
and the night sky is just too beautiful to miss.

Bear, does everything have to change?
Can't some things stay the same?

What Bear Said

Actually, everything IS constantly changing—we are, the mountains and trees are, the sky, the whole earth and Universe. Some changes are so slow we don't even notice. Some are so sudden they surprise us. We can choose to make changes, like how we act or what we pay attention to, but many changes are beyond our control. We can fight them, or we can accept them.

We were walking and came upon an ugly sight...

 Why would anyone leave their trash here, Bear?

What Bear Said
It's sad, no one has taught them to love and respect our beautiful earth. They don't understand they are hurting... their home.

Later that day we saw smoke and heard strange sounds…

Bear, what is that?

What Bear Said

It's some men and their machines cutting down trees to make lumber for building. Let's hope they take from the forest only what they need with loving care, so enough is left for all the critters and woods to stay wild, healthy and beautiful!

People must work together with the earth and not let greed or carelessness destroy the balance of life.

Meaning & Purpose

Bear, what is this all about? Why are we here? What am I supposed to do? I really just want to play a lot and have fun!

What Bear Said

Well, yes, we ARE here to play. Look at our beautiful playground! AND, we have to eat, and stay warm (pick berries and find a den), and that takes some work. The tricky part is keeping it all balanced.

What is this really all about? It is The Great Mystery. Many ideas have been shared, but no one really knows for sure. Perhaps we are close to the answer when we are feeling the happiest, when we have found our "place in the woods," have loved ones who love and appreciate us, and when we have found our unique gifts—those things we are good at and have passion for—and are offering them to the world.

Bear, it seems to me the most
important thing is
KINDNESS.

Us big critters need to be kind to the little ones and watch out for them... to remember, no matter how big or small we are, we need each other.

Bear, could we pick some more berries?
I'd like to put some out for Badger to find.

What Bear Said
That's a very kind idea. Yes, let's pick some berries. By the way, you have been listening and learning very well.

What was that, Bear? I wasn't listening!

What Bear Said
Ha! Ha! Very funny!

Many years later...

Bear and I have continued to have many conversations since those early years. Now I am old. My children and grandchildren are grown. I have introduced them to Bear indirectly, and our conversations go on...

I'm glad you're still here, Bear. I haven't outgrown my need for your wisdom... and now there's another one here I'd like you to meet.

What Bear Said

You keep drawing and I'll keep showing up.

Well, hello, little one...

Bear, I have a few questions...

Gratitude

Thank you to all my teachers and healers. Thank you to all who read rough drafts and who encouraged me to create this book. Special thanks to Jeff, my son, who gave in-depth and valuable critiques of my first drafts, as well as Stacey, my daughter, whose thoughtful insights were very helpful.

Thank you to CJ McLaughlin for helpful edits and encouragement, Sandra Wheeler, Pat Righter, Bill Kauth, Bets Snyder, Janet Taylor , Hector Aleman and Daniel Sperry for continual encouragement to make this book a reality.

Also, thanks to Margaret Loken for valuable feedback and encouragement and other members of the poet's group who have taught me about wordiness.

A big thank you to the Haines and Friends Foundation who awarded me a grant to help in the creation of this book.

Lastly, but certainly not least, thank you to Patty Arnold who designed the book and made each page look so much better.

Jack Wiens has illustrated over 40 children's books for self-publishing authors. He was also a professional counselor for 33 years. He has enjoyed being father to a daughter and son and "Pa" to three grandchildren who are all now grown.

He enjoys tennis, biking, hiking and exploring the Oregon coast and whale watching. His home is Ashland, Oregon, about 150 miles from Lakeview, Oregon, where he was born. Visit him on www.jackwiens.com.

Also by Jack Wiens: **Tending Our Grief** available on Amazon. https://a.co/d/1c8iekR

Printed in the USA
CPSIA information can be obtained
at www.ICGtesting.com
JSHW072337061124
72978JS00010B/16